QUEST of the GODS

With thanks to Martin Howard

First published in the UK in 2013 by Usborne Publishing Ltd.,
Usborne House, 83-85 Saffron Hill, London EC1N 8RT, England.
www.usborne.com

Text copyright © Hothouse Fiction, 2013

Illustrations copyright © Usborne Publishing Ltd., 2013

Cover and inside illustrations by Staz Johnson.
Map by Ian McNee. Coffin illustration by David Shephard.

With thanks to Anne Millard for historical consultancy.

The name Usborne and the devices ♀ ☻ are Trade Marks of
Usborne Publishing Ltd.

A CIP catalogue record for this book is available from the British Library.

ISBN 9781409562023   JFM MJJASOND/13 02927/1
Printed in Dongguan, Guangdong, China.

INTO THE UNDERWORLD

RISE OF THE HORNED WARRIOR

DAN HUNTER

USBORNE

The Sacred Coffin Text of Pharaoh Akori

I shall sail rightly in my vessel
I am Lord of Eternity
in the crossing of the sky.

Let my heart speak truth;
Let me not suffer
the torments of the wicked!

For the Great Devourer awaits,
And the forty-two demons
howl around the Hall of Judgement.

Let me hold my head upright in honour,
and be spared the claws and teeth
of the Shrieking Ones.

The Eaters of Bones,
let them not touch me.
The Drinkers of Blood,
let them not come near me.
The Winged Ones with Jaws of Iron,
may they pass me by.

And may I remain safe
in the presence of Osiris forever.

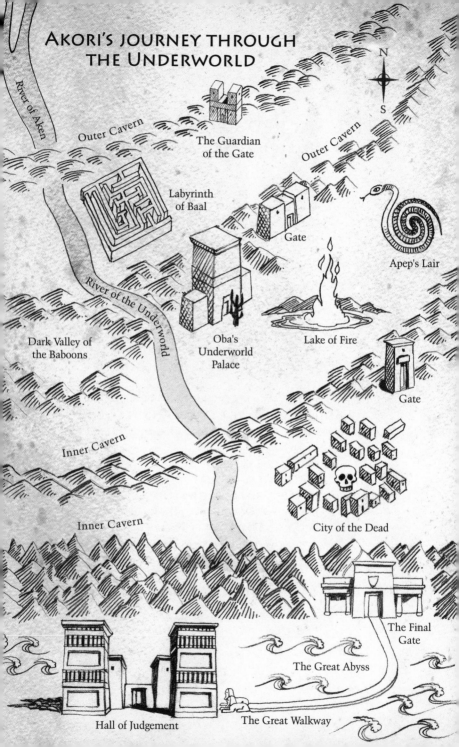

PROLOGUE

The storm howled through the bleak palace, carrying with it the foul stench of the Underworld. In the palace hall, torches made from human bones burned wildly. Their sinister light flickered upon the monstrous faces of the statues all around. With a clap of thunder a chill wind swept into the hall. It rustled the robes of the demon-boy, Oba, sitting stiffly on a vast black throne.

Oba, once the Pharaoh of the great lands of Egypt, now ruled the Underworld. Osiris, the true King of this land, had been imprisoned by Oba's ally, the evil God, Set. But ruling one kingdom was not enough for Oba. He would not be content until he had taken control of all of Egypt once more.

A flash of lightning lit up Oba's face. It was set in an expression of fury. He was thinking – as always – of Akori, the boy who had defeated him and taken his place as the Pharaoh of Egypt. A crack of thunder, even louder than the last, interrupted his thoughts. In the dim light of the fiery torches, Oba looked around. Every surface of the hall was covered in hieroglyphs. Words of dark power crawled across the walls. Pictures of fearsome Gods with human bodies and animal heads glared at him. Then, as another blinding flash of lightning lit up the room, their glares seemed to transform into looks of terror.

Oba frowned. He could hear a terrible rasping sound behind him. A blast of hot air stung the back of his neck and his sweat prickled on his skin.

"Is your plan ready?" a voice growled, more terrifying than death itself.

Oba looked over his shoulder. Set was standing behind him, his jet-black eyes glinting with rage. Since being banished to the Underworld Oba had become accustomed to all manner of evil demons and Gods, but none were so fearsome as Set, the Lord of Storms. He had the towering body of a human giant and the scowling head of a monstrous beast. Oba couldn't help shuddering.

"I wish you wouldn't do that," he said in a bad-tempered voice, trying to disguise his fear.

"Is your plan ready?" Set repeated, striding in front of Oba. The whole hall shook with every step he took.

"Yes," Oba said quickly, gripping the arms of his throne. "But what about your part of the bargain?"

Set's eyes gleamed from black to red.

"Every day I have Osiris imprisoned, his power drains like the blood from a sacrificial pig," he rasped. "The outer caverns of the Underworld are filling with the dead and they are becoming more unsettled and angry by the minute." The Dark Lord gave a fearsome grin, baring his long, sharp teeth. "I have sent some ahead to the land of the living to begin our assault. Soon, we will be ready for the full attack. They will make an unstoppable army!"

"And I will lead them into battle and take Egypt back from that farm boy, Akori." Oba spat out the name of his hated enemy. "I will rule in both worlds. The living and the dead will all grovel before me. I will be greater than any Pharaoh in history."

Set frowned. "But how can you be sure of victory against the farm boy when he has beaten you before?"

Oba's mouth twisted into a snarl almost as ugly as Set's. He smashed his fist into the arm of the throne, causing a thick cloud of dust to rise. "Akori is nothing. A common farm boy. A worm," he shrieked. "He has been lucky, but this time he will not win. This time I have set a trap he cannot possibly survive."

"What is this trap that you speak of?" Set asked.

Oba looked upwards. "Lord Baal, thunder your worst!" he cried. A bolt of lightning lit up the hall.

Set threw his head back and began to laugh. "Ah. You have come up with a fine trap indeed."

Outside, black clouds swirled, spreading across the Underworld. And, as if joining in the laughter, thunder rumbled in the dark sky.

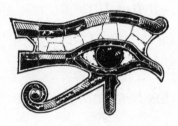

CHAPTER ONE

The Pharaoh Akori looked out of the window of his palace. On the horizon a cluster of dark storm clouds were gathering like an advancing army. Akori gripped the handle of his *khopesh* and frowned. "Oba's power is growing. I can feel it," he said.

As if on cue, a huge bolt of lightning split the sky in two, bathing the palace in a cold, white light.

"I know," said Akori's priest and trusted friend, Manu, as he stoked the fire. "For two days now, this storm has been building and still it doesn't rain. Something isn't right."

The door creaked open. Both boys turned to see the old High Priest of Horus shuffle in. Ebe the cat jumped down from her seat on the window ledge and padded over to him. The old man smiled as the Cat Goddess rubbed against his legs. Even when she had taken the form of a servant girl in his temple, Ebe had never spoken, but she always found a way to make her feelings known. The High Priest bent down to stroke her, but when he stood up again his expression was grave.

"Akori? Are you here?" he asked. Despite his sightless white eyes, the old High Priest's gaze was directed towards Akori, as if he could sense the young Pharaoh watching him.

"Yes, I am here," Akori replied. He strode over to the old man and helped him sit down on one of the benches. Manu came over and sat beside them.

"I'm afraid I have some very troubling news from my friends among the priesthood," the High Priest said.

Akori and Manu stared at him.

"What is it?" Akori asked, placing a hand on his shoulder.

The High Priest took a deep, wheezing breath. "They all speak of the same thing. Sinister noises coming from tombs and burial chambers, moaning and scratching. It is as we feared. The dead are rising."

"Oba," said Manu, his eyes wide. "It has to be. Only the Lord of the Underworld has the power to make the dead walk in the lands of the living."

"Their souls are in torment," the High Priest said. "With Osiris imprisoned, none may be judged and the dead cannot rest.

Oba must be planning to send them against Egypt soon."

Akori imagined a terrifying army of the dead sweeping across the land. It had been bad enough on his last quest when he'd had to fight a gruesome collection of animal corpses after they'd escaped their tombs. But how much harder would it be to stop dead warriors than dead dogs and baboons?

A chill crept up Akori's spine. *No, I will not be frightened*, he told himself silently. *All of Egypt depends on me. I will stop Oba and release Osiris, whatever it takes.* He looked down at his golden coat of armour, given to him by the God Horus – and the red Pharaoh Stone glowing in its collar; the Stone of Courage. He'd won it after defeating Sokar, one of the corrupted Gods working for Oba, ripping the Stone from the belly of the monstrous Guardian of the

Gate. But Horus had said that he must defeat five Gods and win all five of the stolen Pharaoh Stones before Osiris could be freed. Akori got to his feet and began pacing up and down.

"We have to stop Oba before his army of the dead grows too strong," he said. "We have to go deeper into the Underworld. If only Horus would instruct us about our next quest."

Outside there was a mighty crash of thunder, causing the palace itself to shake.

"The God of Thunder certainly seems angry," Manu said, looking towards the window nervously.

Akori peered outside. The dark storm clouds had moved a lot closer now, casting huge shadows upon the land. He touched the Stone of Courage on his collar, and felt new hope flood through his fingers and into

his heart. He turned back to the others.
"We cannot wait any longer," he told them.
"I'm going to summon Horus."

From her seat on the High Priest's lap Ebe
looked at Akori and nodded her pale head.
Akori smiled at her. Ebe might be a small cat
right now, but when she took on her Goddess
form she became a formidable wildcat. Akori
was very grateful to have her by his side.

"Follow me," Akori said.

Together, they walked past giant, carved
pillars of golden stone to a looming statue
of the falcon-headed God, Horus. They all
kneeled at the foot of the statue. Ebe sat
proudly alongside them, her tail curled
around her front paws. Noticing that Manu
was shaking slightly, Akori squeezed his
shoulder. Manu might feel more at home in
the palace library than he was on quests to
battle with evil Gods – but Akori knew that

nothing would stop Manu joining him on their next mission.

Manu flashed Akori a nervous grin, then bowed his head.

Akori closed his eyes and began to pray.

"Lord Horus, Protector of Egypt, hear the prayer of your Pharaoh and champion," he said loudly. "Help me to overcome the enemy who would let evil loose across your lands. Help me to—"

Akori stopped speaking as he heard a scratching noise coming from a stone door set into the wall.

"Horus is coming," said Manu, his voice hushed with awe. "He's answered your prayer."

But, as the scratching became louder, the old High Priest began to frown. "That is not the way Horus would come," he said. "That door leads to..." His voice trailed off as the door began to open.

A quivering hand reached out of the darkness. A hand wrapped in tattered bandages. Rotting flesh hung from the bones. Another hand gripped the edge of the door, wrenching it slowly open. Stone rasped on stone.

"That door leads to a shrine to the royal ancestors!" the High Priest shouted in warning.

The door creaked open. The mummy of the Pharaoh Amenhotep, dead for five hundred years, lurched out of the darkness. Beetles swarmed from his empty eye sockets and gaping mouth. Behind him came two more mummies, their ripped hands reaching blindly.

"They must be his servants," Manu cried.

Akori scrambled up, Manu beside him. At his feet he heard Ebe hissing. His mouth went dry as he looked into the face of Egypt's ancient King. It was impossible to believe that the horrifying figure swaying before him had once been in his position, as Pharaoh of all Egypt. The mummy's bandages were shredded and stained. Scraps of tattered skin flapped from bare bones. Then the festering eye sockets fixed upon him. Hands raised, reaching for Akori's throat, Amenhotep opened his mouth and screamed his rage.

CHAPTER TWO

Before Akori could stop Amenhotep, Manu stepped forward. "I'm in charge of this shrine," he shouted. "How dare you set foot in here without being called. Begone!"

"Manu, *no!*" Akori yelled.

But it was too late. The mummified hand of Amenhotep shot out and gripped his friend by the throat with an unnatural strength. Manu was no longer shouting. All that came from his mouth now was a horrible gurgling sound. His face began to turn the purple of beetroot.

"Leave him alone," Akori bellowed. His fist blazed through the air, carrying with it every ounce of strength in his body. It hit Amenhotep's jaw with a cracking sound, spinning the dead King and sending him flying back into his two groaning servants.

Manu collapsed to the floor.

"Stop this!" the High Priest commanded.

Akori looked over his shoulder. The old man was on his feet and hobbling forward.

"Get away!" Akori shouted as he bent to help Manu up.

But his words were ignored. The High Priest's normally gentle face was transformed. His white eyes burned like ice. "In the name of Horus, I command you to leave this place," he thundered, one hand raised. There was no trace of age in his voice now. This was the voice of a man who had been High Priest for a lifetime. A voice that could not be disobeyed.

The Pharaoh and his servants shuffled back slightly, moaning.

Then they stopped.

Amenhotep laughed.

Akori felt his heart lurch in his chest. Amenhotep's low, rattling chuckle was full of misery.

"Horusss?" said the dead King, in a whisper that sounded like the slithering of worms in the dark. "Horusss doesss not command usss. We sssserve different masssters now."

"Set and Oba," snapped the old priest. "But in life you were a great Pharaoh. Why now, in death, do you serve evil?"

"There isss no choice," hissed Amenhotep. "We mussst obey the Lordsss of the Underworld."

"And what does evil demand?" asked Akori.

Once more Amenhotep's swarming eye sockets turned towards him.

"Kill," the dead Pharaoh groaned, taking a lurching step towards them.

"Get back," Akori said to the old High Priest.

The High Priest stood motionless. "But…"

"That is an order from your Pharaoh," Akori said, carefully circling Amenhotep. His *khopesh* was in his hand, the razor-sharp edge of the golden blade glittering. "Go to the great hall. If we fail, someone must warn the people about Oba's plans."

The old priest nodded, backing away as swiftly as he could manage. "Akori –" he began, as he opened the door – "do not destroy Amenhotep unless you *absolutely* have to."

Suddenly, Amenhotep lunged at Akori, a shower of beetles falling from his mouth.

Keeping the curved sword between them, the young Pharaoh leaped aside with a speed the mummy couldn't match. "Why can't I destroy him?" he shouted to Manu, confused. "I mean, he is already dead."

"Amenhotep's soul has been judged and should be at rest with Osiris," Manu said breathlessly as he fended off one of the mummified servants with a piece of firewood. "Set has wrenched it from the place it belongs and sent it back to its body. If you destroy Amenhotep here, his soul will never find its way back. He will never find peace."

"But he wants to kill *us*," Akori said, ducking as Amenhotep made another grab for him.

"Amenhotep is Set and Oba's slave now, but he is *your* ancestor," Manu gasped, as the servant lunged towards him. "Once

Osiris is released, his soul will return to its
resting place."

Akori frowned. "Well," he said, "if we can't
destroy him, we'll just have to send him back
where he came from." Leaping forward, he
smashed his shoulder into Amenhotep's
chest. "Get back to your tomb!" he shouted.

The dead Pharaoh's fingers clawed at Akori,
gripping his arm and pulling him into a deadly
hug. Rotting limbs began tightening around
him, squeezing the air from his lungs.

"You mussst die," moaned the ancient
Pharaoh.

The smell of death filled Akori's nostrils
as he found himself face to face with his
ancestor. The magical armour Horus had
given him could turn blades and stop arrows,
but it was little good against the crushing
embrace of a mummy.

"Yes, but not today," Akori hissed. His arms

were held tight but his legs and head were free. With an almighty roar he brought one of his knees up into the mummy's stomach.

There was the terrible crunch of breaking bone, followed by a groan. The mummy's grip loosened. Akori whirled around in a low, roundhouse kick that took Amenhotep's legs out from beneath him. The mummy smashed to the floor.

Quickly, Akori glanced around. One of the servant mummies had cornered Ebe. The small cat hissed and spat as the bandaged corpse moaned in triumph. But, just as it bent down to crush the life out of her, Ebe stretched her back. And kept on stretching, until the tiny hissing cat was the size of a lioness. Huge paws landed on the mummy's shoulders. Claws ripped downwards, tearing bandages from paper-thin skin and ancient, brittle bone. The mummy staggered back.

Ebe swatted at the flailing body as if it was a ball of wool.

Then Akori heard a shout from Manu. He spun around just in time to see Amenhotep's other servant attacking Manu, who staggered back against a pillar. Knees folding, he crumpled to the ground as the mummy advanced. Just as it reached for Manu's bruised throat, Akori leaped onto its back. He began raining blows on its head with the hilt of the *khopesh*.

"Touch him again and I don't care what happens to your soul," he yelled as the mummy groaned in frustration, trying to pull him off. But before it could get a grip on him, Akori leaped down. He landed a kick at the base of the mummy's spine that sent it flying into the wall.

As Akori regained his balance he saw Manu gaping in horror at something over his shoulder. Instinctively he ducked at the same time as he whirled round. Amenhotep was standing there, his rotting hands clutching at the empty air where Akori's head had just been.

Akori's muscles tightened as he prepared to leap at his ancestor. He felt the shrivelled fingers of the servant mummy pulling on him from behind. Caught between two attackers he lashed out with his *khopesh*, slicing through the dry bone as if it were air. Howling, the servant mummy fell back, holding a stump where its hand had once been. Akori's stomach turned as he watched the bandaged hand wriggling towards him across the floor. With a quick kick, he sent it flying back through the door. Out of the corner of his eye, he saw Ebe's powerful paws batting the other servant in the same direction. Then, as if to preserve her

Goddess power, she began shrinking back into her smaller form.

Crouching, Akori turned to face Amenhotep again, holding his *khopesh* steadily before him. The dead Pharaoh groaned and started forward. Flashing gold, the sword arced through the air, leaving a gaping slash in Amenhotep's ragged bandages.

"Try it," whispered Akori. "But I'll take you apart and throw you back where you came from, one piece at a time."

"You musssst die," Amenhotep groaned again, lunging forward once more, fingers reaching for Akori's throat.

"Go back to your tomb," Akori shouted. "Or your soul will never find peace again."

"I obey the Lordsssss of the Underworld," moaned Amenhotep, swinging his fist.

Akori dodged it easily. But just as he was

33

about to launch a kick at the Pharaoh mummy, a bolt of lightning shot in through the window. Blinded by the sudden, dazzling light, Akori lost his footing and fell backwards. Manu and Ebe raced to his aid, but when they turned they were greeted with a terrifying sight. The remaining servant mummy was on fire. The air was filled with the pungent stench of his burning flesh.

"He must have been hit by the lightning!" Manu gasped.

The servant mummy let out a blood-curdling cackle and started moving towards them. With every step the flames consuming his body got fiercer and higher, until he'd become a walking pillar of fire. Amenhotep advanced on the opposite side – his withered arms raised, intent on death.

Akori looked around for an escape route but there was none.

"Mussst kill," Amenhotep rasped, from the other side of the flames.

"We're trapped!" cried Manu, as the fearsome mummies closed in to deliver the fatal blows.

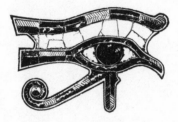

CHAPTER THREE

The flames leaped higher and higher, and began turning from red to gold. Akori shielded Manu and Ebe with his body, but he knew this would make little difference. Soon they would all be burned to a crisp.

Gradually, a figure began to take form in the flames. The tall, muscular figure of a man – with the head of a hawk.

Akori gasped with joy. "Horus!"

Manu, Ebe and Akori watched, awestruck, as Horus stepped out of the fire.

As he did so the column of flames around him spluttered and died. The servant mummy stood before him, his tattered bandages singed black as the night sky. Amenhotep took a step backwards.

Then Horus spoke, his voice as clear and deep as summer skies. "What is this? Who dares attack my champion?"

The mummies swayed from side to side, not making a sound.

Akori stepped forward, and bowed. "Set and Oba, Lord Horus," he said. "They sent the Pharaoh Amenhotep and his servants against us."

"Kill Akori..." Amenhotep groaned. But all of the venom had gone from his voice. He staggered towards Horus and held out his ragged arms in desperation.

"Ssstop me," he moaned, before lurching at Akori once again. "Pleassse,

39

help ussss. Mussst obey. Mussst kill."

Horus laid a gentle hand on the dead Pharaoh's head. "Sleep, faithful servant," the God whispered.

Akori looked into the ragged face of his ancestor. A solitary beetle crawled from one of Amenhotep's eye sockets and scuttled down his face like a black tear. "I am sssorry, my grandson," the mummy whispered. "I had no choice." Half-turning, Amenhotep managed to hiss, "My thanksss to you, Lord Horusss," before he fell to the floor, lifeless again.

"Sleep," Horus repeated, laying a hand on the servant mummy that had been struck by the lightning bolt. The creature fell with a sigh of peace.

"I cannot return them to the afterlife, but I can give them rest until Osiris returns to his throne," said Horus, going to the shrine to bless the other servant mummy. "Nothing will disturb their slumber until then. Place them back in the shrine. Be gentle with them. They have suffered enough already."

When the grisly work of lifting the mummies back into the shrine was finished, Horus nodded his approval.

"You did well. In life Amenhotep was a great Pharaoh. I would not have his soul in torment until the end of days. It is evil magic that Oba casts, dragging the dead from their tombs to attack you. There will be a reckoning when his own soul is judged."

"Or before then if I get my hands on him," said Akori, grimly.

"That time will come soon enough," Horus said with a wise smile. "Now you must leave, my champion. The second part of your quest awaits. As you have seen, Oba and Set grow more dangerous. You must reach the Underworld before sundown and win the second Pharaoh Stone."

"But do I have to win all five Stones?" Akori asked. "Couldn't I just find Oba and kill him now?"

Horus shook his head, his big falcon eyes sparking with intelligence. "You might kill Oba, but Set and the four remaining Gods who serve him would keep Osiris in his prison," he reminded Akori. "The army of the dead would still gather and overrun Egypt. To defeat Oba and Set and stop the army, you must first defeat the Gods who serve them. Win the Stones and you will be strong enough to face both of them."

Akori bowed his head. "Yes, My Lord."

"Return to your tomb in the Valley of the Kings," said Horus. "Quickly, before the sun sets. This time you must go deeper into the Underworld." The God looked into Akori's face. "Take my blessings with you," he said.

Golden light surrounded Horus for a second. Forming a column it flared up towards the roof. Then he was gone.

For a few moments there was silence. It was broken by the voice of the old High Priest. "You heard the God, you'd better be leaving," he said gruffly. They all turned to see the old man standing in the doorway.

Ebe looked up at Akori and Manu, mewing.

"Yes, of course you're coming, Ebe," said Akori with a quick smile. "I wouldn't dare leave you behind." Then he looked at Manu. "Maybe you should stay here this time? You'd be useful here in the palace, too, you know?" Knowing how nervous his friend was about going back into the Underworld, he wanted to give him the choice of staying behind.

Manu stood tall, and folded his arms across his chest. For a moment he looked every inch a High Priest, despite his youth. "You're not going anywhere without *me*," he said firmly. "It's the three of us. *Always*."

The old High Priest looked down proudly on the boy who had been his student. "Wisdom will come with the passing years," he said. "But your courage is already as great as any hero's, Manu."

Manu blushed. "Thank you. I'll keep working on the wisdom," he mumbled.

"Come on then. It's already the afternoon and we've a lot of ground to cover," Akori interrupted. He felt a sudden surge of excitement. Waiting and wondering what was going to happen next had been frustrating. Now he had instructions from Horus for his next quest he could finally do something. Oba and Set had sent Amenhotep to kill him but they had failed. Now nothing would stop him from claiming the second Pharaoh Stone.

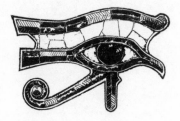

CHAPTER FOUR

Akori and Manu, with Ebe padding between
them, crept out of a small door at the rear of
the palace. Storm clouds blanketed the entire
sky, transforming it into a bleak, black
canopy. But still no rain had come. The wind
was howling, lashing and biting at their
limbs. Keeping to the shadows of the
quietest streets, the trio managed to avoid
the few people who were not sheltering
inside. There was little danger that they
would be recognized. Manu wore the simple

clothes of a lowly apprentice priest, while Akori's golden armour and *khopesh* were hidden beneath a plain dark cloak. He didn't want to take any chances. People would get suspicious if they saw their Pharaoh roaming the streets unguarded and, for now, the exact nature of their mission had to remain secret.

When they arrived at the east bank of the River Nile, Akori headed straight for a boatman.

"How much to take us to the other side?" he called.

A sun-beaten face peered up at them from beneath a makeshift shelter of old cloth tied to wooden stakes. "In this weather?" the man shouted above a rumble of thunder. "You've got to be joking. Come back when the storm clears. I'll take you then if you've got silver."

"I've got copper," said Akori showing the

man a small handful of copper nuggets. As Pharaoh he could have showered the man in gold, but it would be far too suspect for an ordinary citizen to be so extravagant. "We need to go now."

The boatman looked down into Akori's hand. "I don't know," he said grumpily. "It's hardly worth risking my life for."

Akori's heart began to pound. There were no other boatmen in sight. If this one didn't take them across the river they'd never make it to the Underworld in time. He looked up at the sky. It was so dark it was impossible to tell how close the sun was to setting.

Knowing they could be running out of time, Akori drew himself up to his full height and put on his most arrogant voice. "Well, take it or leave it," he said.

Manu nudged him, as if to say, *What are you doing?* But Akori's act paid off as the boatman slowly got to his feet and emerged from his shelter.

"All right then," he said, snatching the copper from Akori's hand.

As soon as they clambered onto the boat, the wind strengthened. Ebe curled into a ball beneath Akori's cloak to protect herself from the churning water. It was no wonder the boatman had been so reluctant to carry them across the river; he groaned with each heave of his oars as he battled against the storm. Eventually after being tossed about like a cork, and much cursing from the boatman, they finally made it to the other side.

As they climbed onto the bank Akori looked ahead at the Necropolis of Waset, the pale tombs jutting from the sand. Above them, the mass of black clouds began spitting fat drops of rain and behind the gloom, Akori could just make out the dying rays of the setting sun.

"Come on!" Akori cried. "We're running out of time!"

As they ran past the animal cemetery, flashes of lightning zigzagged above them and the rain began falling like spears. By the time they reached the Valley of the Kings, the ground was as slippery as oil. Ebe hissed crossly as she struggled to keep dry.

Akori reached the steep hillside leading to his tomb. Turning back to Manu, he shouted over the crashing thunder, "We have to climb now. Think you'll be okay?"

Manu nodded as Ebe began stealthily picking her way up the cliff towards a cave high above. Akori and Manu hauled themselves up the wet rocks. The rain caused small waterfalls to gush around them, soaking them to the bone. Another crack of thunder roared above their heads. Startled,

52

Manu lost his grip, and with a shout of panic he began to fall. Lightning fast, Akori grabbed onto his wrist, guiding his hand to a safe hold.

Finally, the two boys hauled themselves onto the highest ledge, to see Ebe sitting in the dry sand of the cave beyond, washing her ears.

"Don't worry about us," muttered Manu as Akori led the way into the tomb without pausing to rest.

Ebe gave him a look that clearly said, "I was wet, *you* can look after yourself," and trotted along behind.

Akori glanced at his own vast face carved in stone. This was the second time he had visited his future tomb and it still gave him the creeps. But the place where they were going to was creepier by far. For the first time since setting off, Akori felt a wave of fear as he thought of the monsters they'd encountered before. What horrors awaited them in the Underworld this time? He quickly traced his fingers over the Stone of Courage in his collar and was instantly filled with a warm glow of confidence.

"Come on," he said to Manu, nodding at the lid of his coffin.

Using all their strength, the two boys pushed the heavy stone, then clambered inside. Ebe leaped in after them before they lowered the lid and huddled together in absolute darkness. At first nothing happened and Akori's heart sank. Were they too late? Had the sun already set behind the storm clouds? Suddenly the coffin began to shudder. Faster and faster, until every bone in Akori's body rattled. The blood in his veins pulsed in time and in the darkness he began to smile. They had made it. His second quest had finally begun!

CHAPTER FIVE

A blue glow appeared on the stone wall of
the coffin, dimly lighting the faces of Akori,
Manu and Ebe. Akori had been expecting
this. The last time they had plunged into the
Underworld, he and Manu had chanted the
words of power that had begun their journey
into the lands of Osiris. Akori's stomach
lurched as the coffin began dropping like a
rock thrown into a well. Bracing himself for
the landing, he squinted at the stone, trying
to make the words out as they appeared,

grateful for Manu's patient teaching that meant he could now read and write, a little. Even so, many of the strange hieroglyphs were still beyond his grasp. The first words were exactly the same as last time.

"I shall sail rightly in my vessel, I am Lord of Eternity in the crossing of the sky..."

Akori stopped reading. "The next bit is different," he said. "The words aren't the same as before." He pointed at the glowing hieroglyphs. "This one means water, I know that, but what does this say?"

"Labyrinth," Manu answered, peering up at the lid. "It looks like some kind of warning about what lies ahead."

"Battle," said Akori, picking out another word. "Battle and water and labyrinth. That doesn't make any sense."

Manu frowned. "You're right, it says that we must fight water and find the fastest path through a labyrinth."

"Fight water?" Akori felt even more confused. "How can you *fight* water?"

Manu shook his head. "Who knows? We're heading into the Underworld, Akori. Nothing is straightforward there."

Ebe pressed her nose against the glowing hieroglyph for water and hissed.

Then the coffin began spiralling even faster. Akori felt his stomach lurch and all of the blood in his body seemed to rush to his head. Just when it felt as if his head might explode, the coffin reached a juddering halt.

Akori looked at Manu and Ebe in the dim blue light. "Good luck," he whispered.

"You too," Manu whispered back.

Ebe nudged Akori's arm with her nose and gave a reassuring purr.

Cautiously, Akori pushed the stone lid back and they all peered out into the gloom.

Rain was falling in sheets. Through the misty air Akori could just make out the open Gate to the Underworld. He shuddered as he remembered what he'd had to do to open it in his last quest – being swallowed alive by the monstrous creature who had guarded the Gate.

"We're back where we left last time," Akori whispered. "On Aken's boat."

Ahead, just visible through the pouring rain, a man sat pulling on a set of black oars, his body facing towards them. His head, however, was facing backwards, for ever looking in the direction the boat was headed. Scrambling out of the coffin, Akori, Manu and Ebe stood at the side of Aken's boat, shielding their eyes from the driving rain. Overhead, lightning ripped through the sky, and thunder rumbled like the warning growl of a dog the size of a house.

"Do you think this is the water we're supposed to battle?" Akori shouted over the deafening roar of the rain.

Manu shrugged. "The warning on the coffin wasn't clear. But let's hope so. It's a fierce storm, but at least it's not actually trying to kill us."

Suddenly, Ebe jumped up, placing her paws on the edge of the boat, ears flat against her head. Gazing out into the rain-lashed darkness, she mewed. Both boys turned their heads to look in the same direction.

"There!" shouted Akori, pointing. "Reeds. We're close to the bank. We might be able to wade ashore if we jump."

"But we have no way of knowing how deep the water is," Manu said with a gulp.

"Only one way to find out," Akori replied, a determined expression etched on his face.

Without another word, he vaulted over the

side of the boat, gasping as he hit the icy river. He grasped onto the side of the boat, trying to stop it moving away. But the water was deeper than he expected – almost up to his neck. The current wrapped itself around him like a rope and began dragging him downstream.

"Quick, Ebe, over here," he panted. Within seconds, the rushing water and Aken's oars would pull the boat from his fingers and it would be swept beyond his reach. Hissing at the water, Ebe jumped onto his shoulder. "Now you, Manu," Akori called.

Manu muttered a prayer as he leaped from the boat. "C-c-cold!" he shouted breathlessly, half-wading, half-swimming towards the shore.

Akori swiftly followed him. He tried to move faster, but his soaking clothes were heavy and the current clutched at them,

threatening to pull him under. Beneath his feet, river mud sucked at his sandals. Gradually, though, he made his way to the shore, struggling through thick reeds.

Sodden, Ebe jumped to the ground, hissing and looking bedraggled. Manu was in a similar state, his cloak spattered with mud and clinging wetly to him.

"I'm beginning to think I'd prefer to fight something that's actually trying to kill us," Akori shouted. Quickly, he pulled off his own sodden cloak. There was no need for a disguise here and it was too wet to be of any use.

But Manu didn't reply. Instead, he stared past Akori, his face draining of colour and his eyes widening.

"What?" Akori shouted as thunder rumbled again. "What's the matter, Manu?"

Slowly, Manu raised his hand to point.

Akori turned.

His mouth fell open.

Stalking towards them through darkness and rain was the figure of a woman, her robes billowing behind her as if made of mist. Her head was that of a lioness, the muzzle wrinkled in a terrifying snarl, lips drawn back to reveal the deadly fangs filling her mouth.

A roar, loader than the thunder, split the air. The figure threw back her head – and let out a blood-curdling howl.

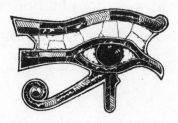

CHAPTER SIX

"It's Tefnut, a Water Goddess," Manu yelled to Akori. "I *knew* it wouldn't just be water we had to fight."

Akori didn't answer. A deep hiss from behind told him that Ebe had changed form again. He felt wet fur brush against him as the giant cat came to stand at his side. Manu came forward to stand by his other side.

There was a flash of lightning and the red Stone on Akori's chest glinted.

Tefnut glared at it and growled. Then she

stared from Ebe, to Akori, to Manu, and stepped forward.

"You are to be punished for daring to oppose Lord Set and Oba, the true Pharaoh of Egypt," she said in a deep voice that echoed like the thunder above. "That punishment is death – and I am the executioner!" She raised a hand. Long, wickedly sharp claws snapped out from the tips of her fingers.

Akori took a step towards her, his *khopesh* held steady, his knees bending into a warrior's stance. "Wise men say it is unwise to shout 'Victory!' until the battle is over," he said.

"Then let's get it over," Tefnut spat. Looking up at the boiling, black clouds above, she screeched, "Rain!"

At once, the torrent of rain increased. Now, every drop felt like a hammer blow.

The torrents of water that fell into Akori's eyes almost blinded him. Through the haze, he just made out the blurry figure of Tefnut before she pounced. Her claws slashed at his face. Akori swiftly ducked to one side, swinging the curved *khopesh* around with as much speed as he could muster. The blade drew a thin line of blood along the Goddess's arm.

A foul curse filled the air. Snarling, Tefnut threw herself at Akori again. He whirled to dodge her, but this time her claws screeched down the golden armour that protected him.

"Only a coward hides behind armour," growled the Goddess. "Next time, I'll aim for your throat." Tefnut clapped her hands together. "Clouds, do my bidding!" she yelled. Immediately, a thick, black cloud began spiralling down towards Akori like a spear.

68

Faster than a lightning bolt, Akori leaped to one side. The cloud crashed onto the ground where he had been standing, exploding in a shower of water.

Out of the corner of his eye, Akori saw Manu creeping round to circle Tefnut.

"You say he's a coward, but you're blinding him with rain," Manu shouted angrily.

Tefnut whirled round to face him, her muscles clenching, preparing to pounce.

"Let's see how you like it," Manu yelled, flinging a handful of wet mud from the riverbank at her.

Tefnut snarled horribly as the mud smacked into her face. Barely stopping to shake it from her eyes she leaped at the weaponless Manu.

"No!" shouted Akori, jumping forward to protect his friend.

But Ebe was there first. The huge cat hit Tefnut halfway through her leap, smashing her to the ground in a tangle of teeth and claws.

As Akori and Manu ran to help, a roar from Tefnut filled the air. Ebe was thrown back, landing on four paws, hissing and spitting at the evil Goddess. Streaks of blood along her flank showed where Tefnut had clawed her.

Akori let out a gasp. The speed with which Ebe had been beaten – even in her Goddess form – was astonishing.

Overhead, thunder rumbled. A fresh downpour rattled against Akori's armour. *She's too fast*, he thought to himself. *To beat her, I'll have to be even faster.*

He lifted the golden armour over his head. Although it was light and flexible, its weight did slow him down. He placed the armour on the ground. "Who's a coward now?" he called.

Tefnut spun around, snarling and spitting at Akori. Tiny rivers of water ran down his bare chest and onto his soaked linen kilt. He wiped the rainwater from his eyes with the backs of his hands.

"Akori, have you gone mad?" Manu gasped.

A hungry grin spread across Tefnut's ion face. "Maybe you do have some courage, little Pharaoh, but it doesn't matter: you're still going to die." And with that, the Goddess pounced again.

Akori dodged, grunting as her claws grazed his cheek. He leaned back and spun round. The *khopesh* flashed through the air, marking Tefnut with a wound of her own – a stripe of blood across her shoulder.

Snarling, Tefnut made another furious pounce, causing Akori to stagger backwards.

With a cry of triumph, the Goddess was

on him. Akori's move had been a trick though. As she landed, Akori raised his feet and used the power of Tefnut's leap against her, adding an extra push that sent her flying over his head. Yowling, she landed in a crumpled heap.

Limping slightly, Ebe stalked forwards, her golden eyes glowing. Manu also moved towards them, armed with a large rock.

"Leave her to me," Akori panted, scrambling to his feet and raising his *khopesh* as Tefnut sprung up again.

"When I've finished with you, little Pharaoh," spat the Goddess, as she circled him, "I'm going to kill your friends, as slowly and as painfully as I can!" But she seemed a little more wary now, watching Akori as if he was a mouse that had unexpectedly bitten her.

Akori felt rage flood through him. There was no way this spitting, clawing monster was going to harm his friends. Not bothering to reply, he darted forward, swinging the *khopesh* clumsily on purpose. As Tefnut leaped to meet him, he ducked to one side with the speed and agility of an acrobat.

The Goddess yowled in confusion and frustration as her claws met nothing but empty air. Akori shot like a comet to her unprotected side.

Tefnut whirled around, but she was too late. Akori's *khopesh* moved so fast it made a buzzing sound as it spliced through the air and into the Water Goddess.

Her yowl was cut off, sharply.

As angry thunder rumbled above, Tefnut's body spattered into a million tiny drops of water.

Finally, the torrential downpour of rain stopped.

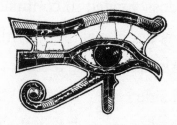

CHAPTER SEVEN

Ebe had shrunk back to her normal cat-sized self again and was licking her wound. Manu crouched beside her, peering at the gash in her side. "It doesn't look too bad," he said softly. "I have some herbs back at the palace that will heal it in a few days. Are you all right to carry on?"

Ebe stopped licking, tilted her head to one side and gave him a look that said, "Of *course* I am." Then she rubbed herself affectionately against his outstretched hand.

"She's not too badly hurt," Manu said, looking up at Akori.

"Thank Horus!" Akori answered, relieved. He pulled his golden armour back on and looked down at the collar with a sigh. Only the red Stone twinkled there.

"Horus said that to win each Pharaoh Stone I had to defeat one of the Gods working for Set and Oba," he said with a frown. "I defeated Tefnut, but won nothing."

"I know," said Manu, looking up at the sky, where black clouds continued to swirl. "And why hasn't the storm gone?"

"We'd better keep going," Akori said. "But which way should we go?"

Manu stood up and both boys looked around. They realized they were standing at the edge of what seemed like an endless desert. The sand was a dark charcoal grey, carved by the wind into threatening waves that reared above their heads. Rocky outcrops jutted from the sand like rows of rotten teeth. Strange cacti dotted the gloomy landscape, thorny trunks twisted into evil-looking faces. A featherless, fleshless vulture took to the air, and began circling above them.

It's waiting for us to die, Akori thought with a shiver.

"Where are we?" he asked.

Manu shrugged. "We could be anywhere. I've never seen a map of the Underworld, but I suppose it's similar to Egypt. Once you leave the river it's mainly desert."

Akori looked down at the grey sand. As the wind whipped around them, it sucked the grains into images of howling faces. He shuddered and looked away. They had to move fast. They had to find the labyrinth –

that must hold the clue to the second
Stone.

"Come on!" he said, trying to sound as
positive as he could, as he put on his damp
cloak. "The coffin dropped us close to where
we needed to be last time. Hopefully the
labyrinth isn't too far from here."

With Ebe trotting along beside them,
the two boys headed into the desert.

Akori tried to move as fast as possible,
but the ground kept tugging at his feet. It
was as if the howling faces in the sand were
trying to swallow them alive. The endless
thunder was louder now too. To Akori's ears
it sounded like wicked laughter, mocking
their efforts.

At last, they reached the edge of a dune.
Ahead was a wall of jagged black rock. Before
it stood a tall obelisk that looked as if it had
been cut from the same stone.

"Maybe it will tell us the way," Akori shouted. Eager to get out of the forbidding desert and the storm, which was building again, he half-ran, half-slid down the dune, sand billowing behind him.

Seconds later, all three of them were standing before the obelisk. Hieroglyphs had been cut into the stone. With a surge of excitement, Akori saw the same symbol for "labyrinth" that Manu had pointed out on the wall of his coffin earlier.

"The Labyrinth of Judgement," shouted Manu above a boom of thunder that shook the ground beneath their feet. "But where is it?"

A jagged fork of lightning lit up the desert for a second.

"Look," Akori replied, pointing to a crack in the wall of rock. "Do you think that could be the entrance?" He began running towards it, Manu panting behind him.

Akori peered into the crack. A dark, narrow passageway lay ahead. In the dark of the storm it was impossible to see where or what it led to. There was another colossal roar of thunder.

"Come on," Akori said over his shoulder to Manu and Ebe. "Let's go in."

"But what if it isn't the entrance?" Manu said.

Akori turned to him and shrugged his shoulders. "Well at least we'll get out of the storm."

Ebe mewed her agreement and slipped inside the rock. The two boys followed. The walls of the passageway were damp and cold. Akori felt the hairs on the back of his neck begin to prickle. What if this wasn't the way to the labyrinth? What if this was some deadly trap laid by Oba and Set? What if he was leading his friends to their death?

Ebe gave a loud mew and began scampering ahead.

"What is it?" Akori called. "What can you see?"

Racing after the cat, Akori saw a pale glow at the end of the passageway. Heading towards the light, they came out on the other side of the rock face into a gaping valley. And there, in the centre, was a labyrinth. It was as white as chalk, and as they got closer, Akori saw why. The walls were made entirely from bones and topped with human skulls.

Akori cautiously peered through the looming entrance to the maze. He couldn't help thinking of the last time he had been trapped in a labyrinth. It had been in Set's temple and he had been chased by a fire-breathing demon. He wasn't sure which was worse – the deathly demon or the rows of skulls leering down at him now through their hollow eyes. Who knew what dangers awaited them this time?

Akori felt for the Stone of Courage on his collar and bravery surged through his veins. He looked at the three passageways facing them. "Let's try the left," he said, beckoning to his friends. But the passage led them straight into a dead end.

They turned and retraced their steps, this time going to the right. But once again they found themselves at a dead end – and the menacing skull of a crocodile glowering down at them.

Akori could feel frustration beginning to bubble away inside him. The coffin text had said that they had to get through the labyrinth quickly. How were they going to do that when every path they chose ended in a wall of dry bones?

"It has to be the centre passageway," he said. "Come on." Akori began running back as fast as he could, his heart pounding in time with his feet as they hit the dusty floor. High above them, thunder continued to roar.

They turned into the central passage and were finally able to begin working their way into the labyrinth. But it wasn't long before they reached another point where the passageway split into three. Akori's heart sank. How much more time would they waste chasing up dead ends? But then he had an idea.

"Let's take one passageway each," he said to Manu and Ebe. "As soon as you reach a dead end, call out –" he glanced down at Ebe – "or *mew* out to the others. When two of us have called out, we'll know that the third person has gone the right way. Then that person can wait for the others to catch up."

With this new way of working they were deep inside the labyrinth in no time.

"Won't be long now," Akori called to the others. "We'll be out of here and—"

An almighty crack of thunder caused the ground to quake and Akori was thrown to his knees. As Manu and Ebe came running towards him, a bolt of lightning hit the wall a few steps away. The dry bones burst into flame, showering sparks into the dark sky.

Akori leaped to his feet. "Quick!" he yelled, grabbing Manu's arm and pulling him along a passage away from the fire. Ebe raced ahead of them.

"But what if this is the wrong way?" Manu cried, his face pale with fear.

"We've got no choice," Akori shouted over the crackling of the burning bones.

"The fire's blocking our way back. Our only way out is to keep going in."

Akori shielded his face from the heat and prayed that he wasn't leading them all into another dead end. Now he knew what the writing on his coffin wall had meant. They had to find the fastest path through the labyrinth – or else be burned alive...

CHAPTER EIGHT

Still dragging Manu by the arm, and with
Ebe racing along beside them, Akori ran for
his life. Behind them, the crackling wall of
fire hungrily devoured everything in its path.
It was even louder than the thunder above.
Without thinking, Akori turned left, then
right, then right again and, when the
passageway split into three, took the centre
passage. There was no time to try and work
out which might be the correct way through
the labyrinth. Akori only knew that they

had to get away from the fire.

He groaned, skidding to a halt. Ahead was another dead end. There was no choice but to go back. He turned and peered along the passage. By the light of the roaring inferno, he spotted another path he'd run past without seeing. The wall of flame was already leaping towards it. Knowing there were only moments before it would be too late, he forced his legs to move again.

"Wait!" Manu said with a cough. "The smoke, it will choke us."

Akori heard a ripping sound. He glanced back to see Manu tear a strip of cloth from his robe and hold it out to him.

"Put this over your face," Manu spluttered. "Ebe, come to me so I can shield you."

Ebe leaped into Manu's open arms and he gently folded her into the front of his robe.

Akori frowned. The fire was now even closer. As soon as Manu had placed a strip of cloth over his own face, Akori shouted, "Now!" His legs powered towards the new passage, racing against the fire. Never had he moved so fast. Feet pounding, ignoring the heat of the blaze, he focused on reaching the path that might lead them to safety.

Immediately the bone wall behind them burst into flame. Akori's heart sank. *Think*, he told himself desperately. There *had* to be a way to beat the labyrinth.

Suddenly, he heard a cry. Whirling round, he saw that Manu had fallen and was trying to stagger back up. His face was creased in pain.

"I've twisted my ankle," Manu cried as he limped forward. Beside him, a shower of sparks flew from the wall of bones as it ignited, causing the skulls on top to explode.

In half a second, Akori was by Manu's side. Putting his arm around him, he ran forward again, dragging Manu clear as the wall fell in a roar of flames. The heat was more intense than ever. Akori took a sharp breath of smoky air. The strips of cloth offered little protection. It felt like his lungs were on fire.

"Lean on me," he ordered, coughing.

"No!" Manu exclaimed. "I'll slow you down. Take Ebe and keep going."

"Never!" Akori gripped his friend round the waist and forced him to carry on.

Think, he told himself again.

The answer came to him in a flash. *Cheat*.

"Manu," he shouted. "I can get us through this, but I'll need your help. Do you think you can carry my weight for a few moments?"

Wide eyes flickering in the firelight, Manu nodded.

Akori looked down at Ebe. "We need your Goddess powers," he said. "Have you the strength to help us? Can you lean against the wall, as high as you can, with Manu standing on your shoulders?"

Ebe nodded her silky head and arched her back higher and higher. Then, when she was fully grown, she stood on her hind legs and rested her huge front paws on the passage wall.

Akori turned to Manu. "Now you, Manu."

As Manu climbed up Ebe's back, grunting in pain as his ankle wobbled, Akori glanced over his shoulder. The fire was so close. They had a minute at most. He opened his mouth to tell Manu to hurry then closed it again, knowing Manu was climbing as quickly as he could.

"This won't take long," he shouted when his friend was in position. "I'll try not to hurt you." Catching hold of Manu's cloak, he pulled himself up onto Ebe's back. Then he clambered onto Manu's shoulders.

Manu gave a low moan of pain.

Akori gripped onto the wall of bones and pulled himself up straight. Trying to ignore the grinning skull next to him, he peered over the top of the wall.

What he saw made him gasp.

The labyrinth was huge, and at least half of it was on fire. Tongues of flame twisted high into the sky, lighting the desert for miles around.

Akori felt Manu's shoulders sag a little beneath his feet. Reminding himself that he had to work fast, Akori gazed over the labyrinth. In the distance he saw a break in the wall that led out into the desert. The exit!

His heart pounding, Akori's gaze followed the twisting, branching passages back to

where they were standing. He had found their way out.

Akori slid back down to the ground. The fire was getting closer every second. He looked at the white-faced Manu and grinned. "Second left, first right, second right, third left. Then follow the centre passage all the way to the exit."

Clenching his teeth in pain, Manu returned the grin. "Quick thinking," he shouted as thunder rumbled again. "No wonder I never beat you in riddle competitions."

Ebe carefully lowered herself onto all fours and looked at Akori. Then she gestured at her back with her huge head.

"You'll carry us?" Akori said.

Ebe nodded and Akori leaped on to her back behind Manu.

As Ebe began to bound along the passageway, Akori repeated the directions over and over, terrified he might forget them.

At last the exit from the labyrinth appeared.

In front of Akori, Manu cried out again. But this time it was in joy and relief, not pain. Ebe raced out into the grim desert. Then they all fell, exhausted, onto the black sand. Turning back, they watched as the last of the labyrinth was consumed by flame.

As Ebe shrunk back to her small cat form, Manu shook his head.

"That was way too close," he said with a sigh. "I never, ever want to set foot in a labyrinth again!"

Akori nodded and smiled. "Me neither." But as he looked down, his smile turned to a frown. "Look," he said, pointing at his collar. "We've fought water and made our way through the labyrinth. But I still don't have the second Stone."

But Manu said nothing. His eyes were wide with fear.

"Manu?" Akori asked.

"I don't think Tefnut was the only water God we have to fight," Manu whispered.

Akori turned.

At the top of a nearby sand dune stood an enormous bull. It was pawing at the ground, sending up thick grey clouds of sand. It snorted angrily and tossed its great black head. Horns as long as Akori's arm and as sharp as daggers glinted in a sudden flash of lightning.

But that wasn't the worst of it.

A huge man was standing on the great beast's back. He was broad and muscular and wearing a helmet with two great horns as fearsome as the bull's, one on each side. Black hair blew around his face and a pointed beard forked down from his chin.

The warrior raised a fist. Blinding light crackled around his fingers. In his hand appeared a blazing, twisting bolt of lightning. He screamed a blood-chilling battle cry in a booming voice that sounded like thunder. The sky roared in answer, great jags of lightning crackling across the clouds.

And there, around his neck, glinted a bright green Stone. Without a word, Akori climbed to his feet, hand reaching for the *khopesh* at his hip. Finally, he had reached the purpose of his quest.

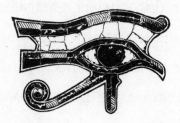

CHAPTER NINE

"Who – *what* – is that, Manu?" Akori shouted as the man on the bull raced towards them down the steep sand dune.

"Baal," Manu replied in a terrified voice. "The Thunder God of Syria. He Who Rides on the Clouds. The Prince of Demons. He's—"

"Silence!" the God roared, brandishing his spear.

Manu went to speak, but no sound came out.

Baal glared at Akori and mini lightning bolts flashed in his eyes. "You might have beaten my ally, Tefnut. And you might have escaped my attack of fire, but you will *never* defeat *me!*" the God roared.

"He's at least a hundred times more powerful than Tefnut," Manu whispered.

As if hearing Manu's words, the massive warrior bellowed his unearthly battle cry again. In the clouds above, thunder echoed his roar. The bull bucked beneath Baal as he flung the thunderbolt.

The blazing spear burned through the air straight at them.

"Scatter!" Akori yelled. He shoved Manu in the opposite direction, as Ebe darted away. Akori threw himself as far as he could.

The ground heaved as the thunderbolt smashed into it where the three of them had been standing just a moment ago. As Akori

fell, red-hot sand rained down on him.
Dazed, he threw his arm across his face
to protect his eyes from the bolt's blinding
light.

The sound of hooves crunching on sand
quickly brought him to his senses. Blinking,
Akori opened his eyes to see the charging
bull almost on top of him. Standing on its
back, Baal screeched an order. Sand billowed
around its hooves as the snorting black beast
increased its speed.

Akori tried to crawl out of the way, but
there was no time. The hooves of the huge
bull were too close.

But then a pale shape flashed out of the
desert. It launched itself at the bull's head
in a hissing whirl of claws and teeth.

Although Ebe was still in her smaller form
she managed to rake at the bull's eyes with
her claws. Tossing its head and screaming,

the bull veered away from Akori. Blinded, but going too fast to stop, its legs buckled. It threw up a huge cloud of sand as its massive weight crashed to the ground.

"Ebe!" Akori yelled, terrified that she had been crushed.

As the sand settled, Baal rose smoothly to his feet. A long, gleaming spear glinted in his hand. He took a step forwards, cursing again as he prepared to strike. Right in front of him, Ebe was scrabbling free from beneath the stunned bull. She was at Baal's mercy.

"I'll kill you!" Akori heard a voice cry. As he threw himself at the Thunder God, he realized it was his own.

Baal's head turned. A blood-chilling smile crossed his face. "You are the one that Set told me about," he said, bringing his spear up. "You are the one who must die." When he spoke, thunder roared above.

Akori let the *khopesh* reply for him.
The curved sword swept through the air in
a golden blur as he struck.

Baal's grin widened. With the speed of
lightning, he brought up his own spear,
turning Akori's blow. "If that is the best you
can do, I will kill you more easily than I
expected."

Unable to help himself, Akori stepped
backwards. Baal stared down at him through
fierce, blazing eyes. As the God raised his
spear again, Akori felt a chill of fear run
down his spine.

Suddenly, Manu ran at Baal, hitting him
from behind with a broken branch. "You'll
have to kill me first," he cried through
gritted teeth.

Baal spun round. "And I will do so with
pleasure, little priest," he laughed, lashing
at Manu with his spear.

Akori managed to block the blow with his *khopesh*. "Manu, get away. Run!" he shouted.

"I'm...sorry...but I can't do that," Manu grunted, swinging the branch again.

Baal's smile faded as it caught him in the stomach. "Enough of this," he spat. With fearsome speed, he attacked Akori – a flurry of blows that sent him reeling away. At the same time, the towering God reached up and clicked his fingers. Lightning crashed as his bull clambered to its feet, already turning to face Manu, its horns lowered, front hoof pawing at the ground.

Scrambling backwards as blow after blow rained down on him, Akori blocked and parried with the *khopesh* as fast as he could. But Baal was faster, and stronger. Three times the God's spear clashed on his armour, knocking the air from Akori's lungs.

Breathless, tired and afraid, Akori fought on. As he jumped back from the deadly point of Baal's spear, he caught a glimpse of his friends. The bull was charging at Manu, but Ebe jumped onto the beast's face and stopped it again. Manu picked up the branch and smashed it into Baal's back. For a split second, the God teetered off balance. Akori saw a chance. Summoning up every ounce of strength, he dashed forward, striking with the speed of a cobra. The *khopesh* sang as it whipped through the air.

Although the God caught the blow on his spear it caused him to stumble backwards.

Akori's heart leaped. Using both hands, he swung the *khopesh* again, praying that this time it would connect.

But Baal recovered. Dodging Akori's blow, he laughed again as his spear lashed out and cut through the branch Manu was holding.

Manu's eyes widened as his broken weapon fell onto the sand.

"Not bad," Baal chuckled, turning to Akori again. "For a moment I almost believed you were a warrior. It was just a moment though." His chuckle turned to a snarl as he launched himself into a fresh attack.

The God's spear seemed to be everywhere at once. With a speed he barely knew he was capable of, Akori parried and blocked. Weapons clashed beneath the swirling clouds, showering the sand in sparks. With sweat running into his eyes, Akori forced his sword arm to move faster and faster but, for all his size, Baal moved like lightning. A massive overhead swing sent Akori to his knees. Once again, Baal roared his battle cry, sensing victory was close.

"Courage, Akori. Courage!" Manu yelled, urgently.

Yes. Of course. I had forgotten, Akori thought suddenly. *Thank you, Manu.*

At the last possible moment Akori brought his *khopesh* up. Baal's blade smashed into it with a God's strength. Akori's arm burned with juddering pain. It felt like every bone was about to splinter. But – somehow – he managed to stop the killing blow.

At the same time the fingers of his free hand reached up and found the Stone on his chest. Red light flared as the gem came alive. A great surge of power flooded up his arm, swelling his heart. Suddenly, he felt as brave as a lion.

He swung the *khopesh* at the God with new energy.

Baal leaped back, dodging Akori's cut with a snarl. Spinning, he thrust again with blinding speed.

Akori's mind was blazing. He knew he

would never beat the warrior God in a straight fight – Baal was too strong and too fast. But there had to be a way to win. Glancing around, he saw Baal's thunderbolt still smouldering in the sand where it had landed. In a flash, an idea came to him. Ducking beneath a lashing cut of Baal's spear, Akori crouched and kicked out, every muscle in his body straining to power the surprise blow.

Baal's legs buckled where Akori struck them and he fell heavily onto his back. He raised his spear to protect himself from Akori's attack.

The attack never came.

Instead, Akori snatched the green Stone from around the God's neck and slotted it into his collar.

"Ebe! Manu! Follow me," he yelled.

Baal staggered to his feet, laughing again.

"You will never run fast enough to escape me, cowardly human," he roared.

"Maybe I won't need to," Akori muttered. He touched the red Stone of Courage with one hand, then dived for Baal's thunderbolt with the other. He could feel power humming beneath his fingers, but it didn't burn.

"What—?" Baal started forward, a look of panic spreading across his face.

"Too slow!" Akori said, as he hurled the thunderbolt.

CHAPTER TEN

The bolt of lightning streaked past Ebe and Manu, and smashed in front of Baal in an explosion of fire. The God staggered back, hands up to shield his face, as the flames raced around him. Within seconds, he and his panicking bull were trapped by a roaring, leaping ring of fire. The flames swarmed hotter and higher. And then, with a terrifying sizzling sound, they were gone.

"That was amazing," Manu panted as he limped over to Akori's side. "I've never seen anyone move so fast."

As if agreeing, Ebe twined herself around Akori's legs, purring.

Reaching down, Akori stroked her soft fur. As he touched her, Ebe looked up at him and mewed. There was no mistaking the warning.

Something was wrong.

Akori scanned the desert, gasping in shock as he realized how dark it had become. Words that Horus had spoken came back to him in a rush: anyone who stayed longer than one night in the Underworld would never leave. "The sun is leaving the Underworld," Akori groaned. "It must be almost dawn. We have to get out of here."

Manu nodded. "Look," he said, pointing to a distant black line snaking through the sand. "There's the river. If we hurry we might still be able to catch Aken's boat and get back to your tomb before first light."

"What are we waiting for?" Akori cried as he started racing towards the river. But then he heard Manu groan. Akori turned and saw his friend bent over in agony, his face pale.

"I can't run," Manu hissed through gritted teeth, as he clutched his swollen ankle. "I'm never going to make it in time. Listen to me. You saved my life in the labyrinth, but this time you *have* to leave me. Egypt needs her Pharaoh. You have to get out, Akori."

Akori shook his head. "I'm not leaving you, even if it means we all stay," he said quietly.

"But look, there's Aken's boat," Manu replied, pointing to a small dot floating down the river in the distance. "There's only a few minutes left. Please, Akori, run."

Akori turned to Ebe. "Can you take your Goddess form?" he asked the small cat, "and carry Manu?"

Ebe arched her back and let out a low mew. But nothing happened. She tried again, but still she remained small. She shook her head sadly.

"She must have used all of her energy in the labyrinth." Manu's head bowed. "Please, Akori. Just leave me here."

Akori frowned. "No. I am your Pharaoh and I command you to come with us. Now, before we lose any more time." He put his arm around Manu. "Lean on me," he said. "Take the weight off your bad foot."

Head bowed, Manu began hobbling across the sand at a speed that made his face twist with pain, Ebe following closely behind.

"Not far now," Akori said as they reached the top of a sand dune. But as he looked down, he felt his stomach sink. Aken's boat was about to disappear into a tunnel. It had to be the tunnel leading back to Egypt. It would take a miracle for them to reach the riverbank in time to catch it.

Manu groaned. "You could have made it if it wasn't for me," he said, with a sob in his voice. "Why didn't you leave me?"

Akori turned to his friend. "Manu, you attacked Tefnut with nothing but a handful of mud, and Baal with a broken stick trying to save me. You are a greater friend than I could ever have wished for. Do you really think I would abandon you to Oba and Set in the Underworld?"

"And you are a greater Pharaoh than any Egypt has ever known..." Manu's voice trailed off. Hope flickered in his eyes as he looked at Akori's collar. "The Stone," he whispered. "You got Baal's Stone."

Akori nodded.

Manu leaned closer, drinking in every detail of the magical gem. His eyes blazed with sudden hope. "Baal is lightning-fast. Could this be the Stone of...*speed*."

Akori's eyes widened. "If there's one thing we need right now, it's speed." With trembling fingers, he touched the glimmering green Stone.

Akori's legs shook, as if filled with a sudden power. Looking across the dunes, he took in the rise and fall of the sands, stretching all the way down to the banks of the river. Immediately he knew what to do. Quickly, Akori bent down and picked up Ebe. Then grinning at Manu he held out his cloak. "Hang on to me." He smiled.

Taking a deep breath, Akori stepped off the ridge of the sand dune. He slid down the bank, pulling Manu behind him. At first Akori felt a lurch, as if the ground was collapsing beneath him. He clutched his Stone, eyes closed tight, heart pounding so

hard it felt as if it might leap right out of his chest. Almost instantly a sense of calm swept through him, leaving in its place a peculiar feeling of lightness. He suddenly became aware of the breeze whistling past him, the wind ruffling his hair. He allowed himself to lean backwards, sensing his legs standing still but strong, feet skimming across the sand beneath him. Cautiously, Akori opened his eyes.

He was sailing across the sands like a boat riding a wave, gliding down the steep dunes. Manu's robes billowed out behind them as he clung onto Akori. The young priest was screaming – at first with terror – but then delight.

"It feels as if I'm flying!" he cried. "It's incredible!"

Akori blinked, water streaming from his eyes as the three of them tore along the sand at top speed. Unable to stop himself, he joined in Manu's laughter as his legs swept across the sand, growing ever faster as they reached the riverbank. As they neared the water, the ferryman's boat was so close that Akori could see Aken himself, his body hunched over the oars while his face looked ahead. Akori could even see the coffin, its lid open, waiting.

"Hold on!" Akori yelled, clutching his Stone. With one final burst of speed he leaped across the water, carried by the momentum, bringing Ebe and Manu with him. Akori let out a cry of joy as he fell, head-first, onto the boat. In a noisy tangle of arms, legs and complaining cat, Akori, Manu and Ebe all tumbled into the waiting tomb.

The lid slammed shut.

The coffin shuddered and began to rise.

Outside, the sounds of thunder faded.

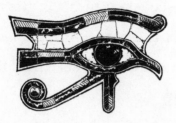

CHAPTER ELEVEN

"… And then Manu attacked Baal with a dried twig," Akori said to the old High Priest with a grin. "It was the bravest thing I've ever seen."

"Ugh, don't remind me," Manu replied, his face draining of colour. "I'm going to have nightmares about thunderstorms for a very long time!"

The old priest ran his fingers over Ebe's silky fur. Manu had spread a paste of rare herbs over her wound and she was now purring contentedly. Above, the sun blazed down on the palace courtyard. "Manu might be brave," he interrupted, with mock sternness, "but a High Priest must be wise. Fighting a God armed only with a stick is most certainly *not* wise."

Manu hung his head in shame. "I'm still working on wisdom," he murmured.

The High Priest's face lit up in a smile that, for a second, made him look young again. He patted Manu on the shoulder. "Wisdom isn't everything, my boy. Sometimes events must be decided by an unthinking act of blind courage. You did well. I am proud of you."

Blood rushed to Manu's face. The High Priest did not give many compliments. "Thank you," he said quietly.

"Still, perhaps you should think twice before throwing mud at Goddesses or poking

Gods with a stick again," chuckled the priest. "That sort of thing does tend to annoy them. You were lucky to escape with only a twisted ankle."

"I'll try and remember," Manu grinned.

"I am proud of *all* of you," the old man said, his face becoming serious again. He turned his white eyes on Akori. "You have won the second Pharaoh Stone." Reaching out with a trembling hand, he touched the green gem.

Akori smiled as the sunlight lit up the magnificent Stones on his collar. He had only been back for a few hours – most of which had been spent in exhausted sleep – but already the adventure seemed like a distant memory. Out here in the palace courtyard with no trace of thunder in the blue sky above and the sounds of street merchants selling their wares on the other side of the wall, the adventure seemed like a strange, unsettling dream.

"Your Majesty, your meal is prepared," said a voice from behind him. Akori turned and saw his chief servant, standing respectfully by a stone table, loaded with every kind of mouth-watering food.

Akori breathed in the delicious smell of the freshly baked bread and the spiced meats. Realizing that it had been more than a day since he had last eaten, he got to his feet and raced to the table. "Thank you," he said eagerly. "Come on, Manu, Ebe, you must be starving." He laughed as Ebe jumped onto the table, licking her lips at the sight of a huge fish.

Taking a deep drink of icy cold, sweet grape juice, Akori sat down, contented. Since he had first found out that he was the rightful Pharaoh of Egypt he'd had very few moments to relax and enjoy himself, but in the courtyard beneath a warm sun, he felt a sudden rush of happiness. "Come on, Manu, what are you waiting for?" he shouted.

Manu was standing close to the pool in the middle of the courtyard, frowning. "I...I thought I heard something," he said, slowly.

Akori walked over to the pool. From far below he heard a deep rumbling moan filled with rage and despair. The surface of the water began to writhe and splash as the groaning grew louder. It was the dead.

The High Priest came to join them. "Your quest is not over yet," the old man said, softly. "The darkness is rising and it seems there is little time for rest."

"I will be ready," Akori whispered.

"And me," said Manu.

Akori heard a mew at his feet. Ebe, too, was ready.

Gratitude swept through Akori. While he had friends like this he could face anything.

Slowly, he raised a hand, his fingertips tracing the three empty spaces on the collar of his armour. Three more times he would have to face Oba's allies. Three more times he would have to fight the dark Gods. Which Gods even Horus could not tell. Then he would still have to face Oba and Set and their dreadful army.

Briefly, Akori closed his eyes. How dare Oba send Egypt's dead against the living? How dare he make slaves of all those people whose souls should be at rest? How dare he threaten the peace and happiness of all Egypt with his endless thirst for power?

How dare he?

Akori's eyes snapped open, blazing with determination. *"I will be ready,"* he repeated.

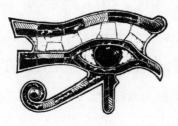

EPILOGUE

*Baal stood, cringing in the dim light of the
Underworld palace. The God's hair and
beard were gone, burned away by the fire.
His skin was blackened and blistered, still
smouldering in places.*

*"Defeated," screeched Oba, as he
circled the cowering figure in front of him.
"You, Baal, Prince of Demons, defeated by
a farm boy!"*

*"My Lords, Oba…Set…" said Baal,
dropping to his knees. His voice rasped,
his throat burned by heat and smoke.*

*"Shut up," screamed Oba, lashing out with
a foot and sending Baal sprawling onto the
floor. "I didn't give you permission to speak,
you miserable failure."*

"Forgive me. I had the boy at my mercy but he…he tricked me."

"I said shut up," snarled Oba, standing over the grovelling God. "God of Thunder? More like the God of pathetic excuses." He paced the floor angrily. "Now Akori has two of the Stones, and it's all your fault." A groan escaped Baal's lips as he struggled back up to his knees. Casually, Set kicked him back down again.

Baal bowed his head. "The boy will not trick me again. Next time I will kill him for certain…" His voice trailed off as Oba began laughing hysterically.

"Next time? Next time?" snarled Set. "You think we'd send a useless weakling like you against Akori again? You're as stupid as you are feeble." The monstrous God leered down at Baal. "Fortunately," he said. "Your failure does not matter. I have a better servant than you. A God who is strong and powerful. A God who is everything you are not. He will crush Akori."

Suddenly, the huge door to the Underworld throne room was flung open, and a cruel, hungry-sounding snarl echoed through it. The doorway darkened as the creature came closer, blocking the scanty light.

On the floor, Baal scrabbled backwards, eyes full of sudden fear. "No, My Lords," he choked. "You go too far. You cannot…"

Set ignored him.

Oba hugged himself, shuddering, as he stared at the creature he knew would finish Akori once and for all.

"Oh yes," Oba grinned. "Akori will never trick his way past you."

DON'T MISS AKORI'S NEXT BATTLE!

SCREAM OF THE BABOON KING

With dark magic invading the land, Akori must seek out Oba's Underworld palace and find the terrifying creature stalking his nightmares – the bloodthirsty Baboon God!

READ ON FOR A SNEAK PREVIEW!

Akori brandished his khopesh. "Remember this?"

"Of course," Oba jeered. "Tell me, have you learned to fight yet?"

"That scar on your chest is a mess," Akori scowled. "It looks like someone's sealed you up with burning tar. What happened to the nice clean wound I left you with?"

Oba's face crumpled into a sneer. "Enough. I'd love to stay and chat some more, but I'm afraid I have urgent work to do. What with preparing my army of the dead and planning the attack on Egypt, I'm a little busy."

"Not too busy to die," Akori shouted, advancing on him. Ebe and Manu followed behind, grim looks on their faces.

"Oh! Speaking of dying, I almost forgot. There's someone you just have to meet!" Oba snapped his fingers.

The doors burst open. Akori stood frozen

to the spot as a monstrous horror came bounding into the room. It was a gigantic baboon, wearing armour and shaking a long club.

To his horror, Akori realized the club had been cobbled together from dead men's bones, a human skull leering at its peak.

"Now I really must go," Oba said, waggling his fingers. "Goodbye, all of you. I'd wish you luck, but there's no point, since you're all going to die."

Oba hastily slipped out of the rear door, closing it behind him, as the baboon craned its huge head down to peer at Akori and let out a bone-chilling howl...

FIND OUT WHAT HAPPENS WHEN
AKORI BATTLES THE MONSTROUS
BABOON GOD IN...

SCREAM OF THE BABOON KING

ISBN 9781409562047

OUT NOW!

COLLECT EVERY UNDERWORLD ADVENTURE:

FIGHT OF THE FALCON GOD

Akori must venture into the dark and deadly Underworld to battle the fearsome Falcon God. But will he make it out alive?

ISBN 9781409562009

CLASH OF THE DARK SERPENT

The Sun God has been captured by the gigantic serpent of the Underworld. Now Akori must defeat the beast, or else darkness will seize Egypt for eternity.

ISBN 9781409562061

DESCENT OF THE SOUL DESTROYER

Akori faces the ultimate challenge as he prepares to battle Ammit, the monstrous Soul Devourer. Can he succeed before Oba's army of the dead destroys Egypt for ever?

ISBN 9781409562085

CATCH UP WITH ALL OF AKORI'S QUESTS!

EVIL PHARAOH OBA HAS IMPRISONED THE GODS WHO PROTECT EGYPT, AND NOW BLOODTHIRSTY MONSTERS ROAM THE LAND. ONLY ONE BOY CAN STOP THEM...

ATTACK OF THE SCORPION RIDERS

For his first quest, Akori must risk his life, fighting giant scorpions and a deadly Snake Goddess. But will his terrifying battle end in victory?

ISBN 97814095621051

CURSE OF THE DEMON DOG

The dead are stalking the living and Akori must send them back to their graves. But dog-headed Am-Heh the Hunter has sworn to destroy Akori...and no one has ever escaped his fearsome jaws.

ISBN 97814095621068

BATTLE OF THE CROCODILE KING

Akori must brave the crocodile-infested waters of the Nile to battle two evil gods – the terrifying Crocodile King, and his gruesome wife, the Frog Goddess – both hungry for his blood...

ISBN 97814095621075

LAIR OF THE WINGED MONSTER

Vicious vultures and deadly beasts lie in wait for Akori as he searches the desert for the Hidden Fortress of Fire – and the Goddess imprisoned there. Will he survive or will this quest be his last...?

ISBN 9781409521082

SHADOW OF THE STORM LORD

The battle to end all battles has begun. Akori must fight Set, the dark Lord of Storms himself, and beat Oba, the evil Pharaoh, to claim his rightful throne. But can Egypt's young hero finally win the crown?

ISBN 97814095621099

FREE GAME CARDS IN EVERY BOOK!

Collect the cards and play the games!

Prepare to launch a full-on
Stat Attack

The aim of the game is to steal your opponents' cards by using the strongest stats from the categories on your cards. Let the battle begin!

Players: 2-4
Number of cards: at least 1 per player
Dice: 1

- Shuffle the pack and deal the cards face down among the players. Roll a dice to see who starts.

- *Player One*: select a category from your topmost card and read out its stat.

- *Other Players*: read out the stat of the same category from your cards. The highest stat wins the "trick", and the winner takes all the cards of the trick and places them at the bottom of their pile. The winner of the last round begins the next by looking at their card, and choosing a new category.

- *DRAW*: all topmost cards are placed in the centre and the same person as in the last round chooses a new category using their next card. The winner of that round obtains all of the cards from *both* rounds.

- *LOSE*: players are eliminated when they lose their last card.

- *WIN*: the winner is the player who obtains the whole pack.

TURN THE PAGE TO DISCOVER EXCITING NEW GAMEPLAY OPTIONS WITH THE PHARAOH STONE CARDS...

EACH BOOK IN QUEST OF THE GODS
INTO THE UNDERWORLD
COMES WITH AN EXCLUSIVE
PHARAOH STONE CARD

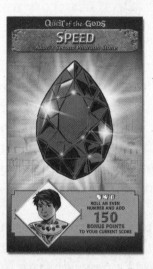

- Each Pharaoh Stone card is worth a number of bonus points. The further in the series you get, the more powerful the Pharaoh Stone card in the book, and the more bonus points available:

  Book 6: Stone of Courage = 50 points
  Book 7: Stone of Speed = 150 points
  Book 8: Stone of Strength = 250 points
  Book 9: Stone of Intelligence = 350 points
  Book 10: Stone of Honour = 450 points